Table of Contents

JACOB OVERCOMES His Fear OF Sleeping Alone

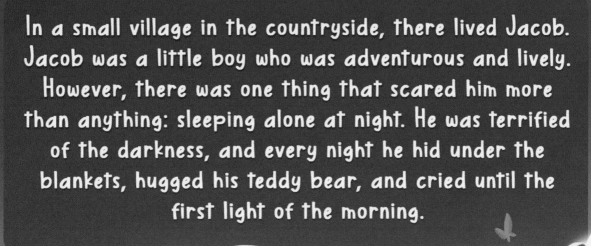

In a small village in the countryside, there lived Jacob. Jacob was a little boy who was adventurous and lively. However, there was one thing that scared him more than anything: sleeping alone at night. He was terrified of the darkness, and every night he hid under the blankets, hugged his teddy bear, and cried until the first light of the morning.

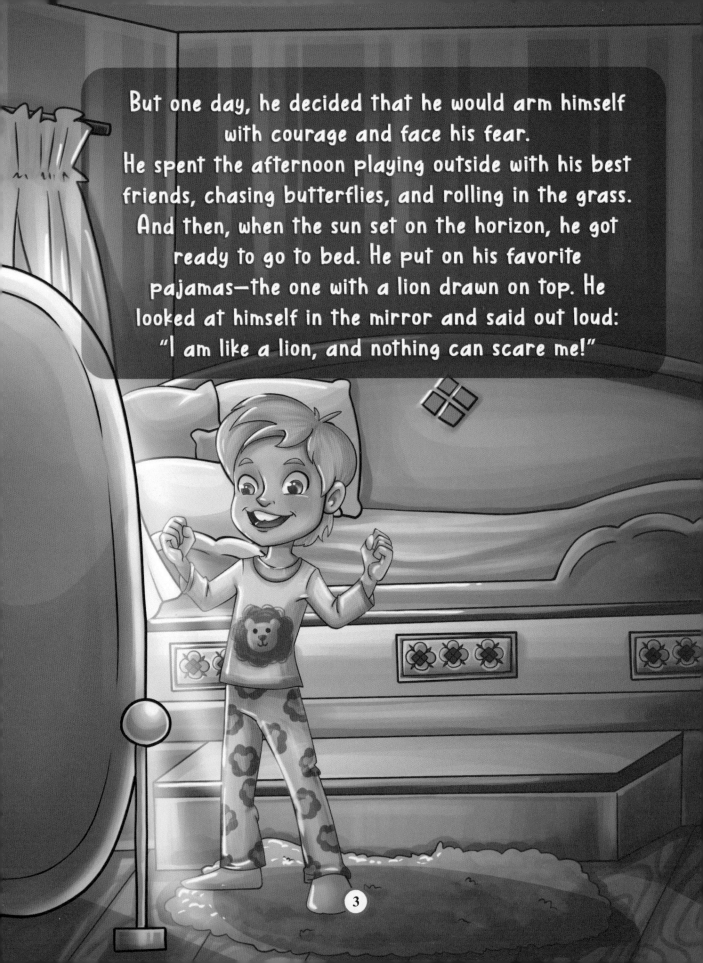

But one day, he decided that he would arm himself
with courage and face his fear.
He spent the afternoon playing outside with his best
friends, chasing butterflies, and rolling in the grass.
And then, when the sun set on the horizon, he got
ready to go to bed. He put on his favorite
pajamas—the one with a lion drawn on top. He
looked at himself in the mirror and said out loud:
"I am like a lion, and nothing can scare me!"

And at that moment, a thrilling bell rang, and, with a puff of smoke, a cute, tiny creature appeared in front of him. The little fairy was glowing in the dark and flying all around the room, laughing happily out loud. Jacob looked at him with his eyes wide open, surprised and full of curiosity.

"Who are you?" Jacob asked him.
"I am Bravy, the Guardian of Courage!" He said with
a squeaky voice. "And tonight, Jacob, I will help you
become a brave little boy!"
"Can you really help me not be afraid to sleep alone?"
Jacob wasn't sure he could trust the little man, but he
was intrigued by this mysterious and friendly creature.
Bravy flew on top of his pillow and sat there
with a big smile.

"Of course, I can! This is why I came. Only if you are ready to face your fears can you really become brave, because courage is like a muscle you need to train. At first, your legs were too weak to carry your weight, but now you can run in the fields all day faster than any of your friends! And the only way to train your courage is to take small steps towards conquering your fears."

"I want to be a brave boy. Show me how I can do it!" Jacob told the funny creature, excited to prove himself.
"Then follow me!" He said, and then he spread his wings and flew outside in the corridor.
"But... It's dark out there, and I'm scared of the dark."
Bravy took him by the hand and looked at him with a big, shining smile.

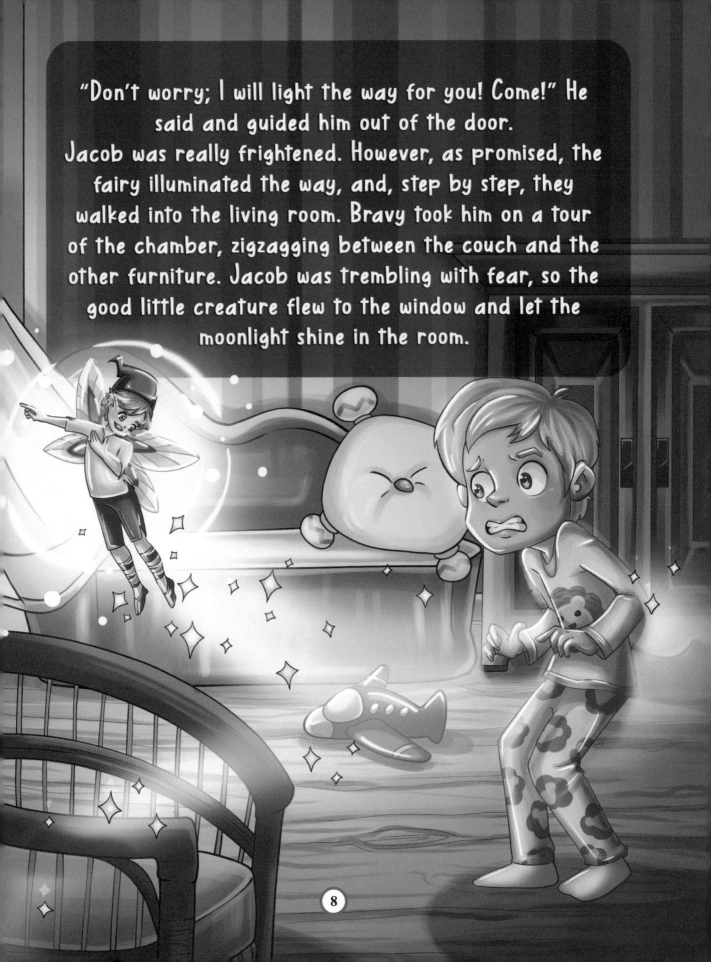

"Don't worry; I will light the way for you! Come!" He said and guided him out of the door.
Jacob was really frightened. However, as promised, the fairy illuminated the way, and, step by step, they walked into the living room. Bravy took him on a tour of the chamber, zigzagging between the couch and the other furniture. Jacob was trembling with fear, so the good little creature flew to the window and let the moonlight shine in the room.

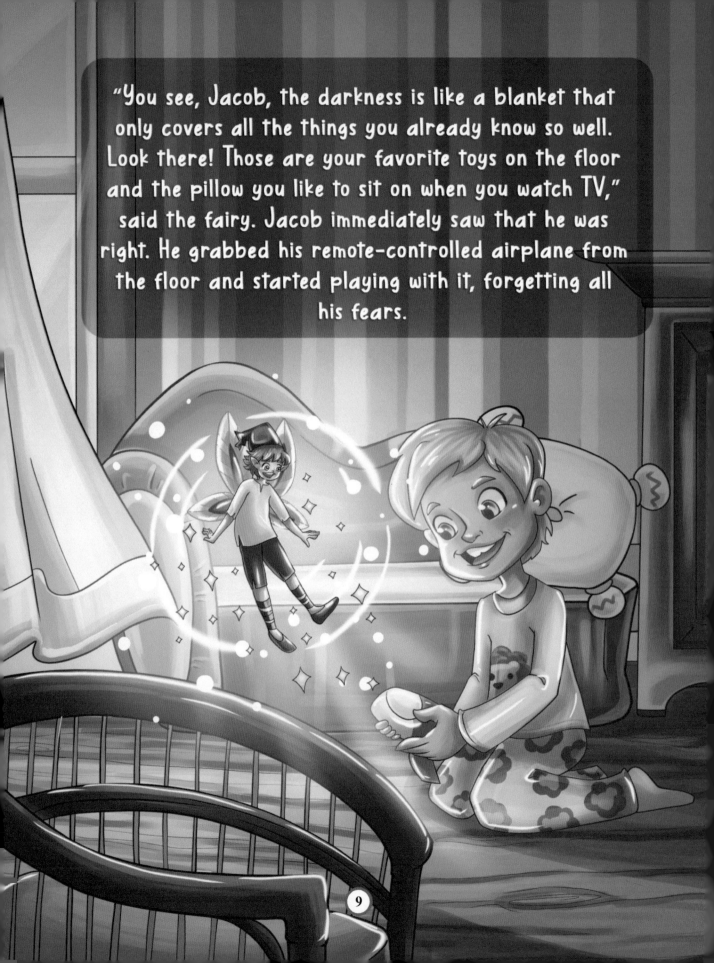

"You see, Jacob, the darkness is like a blanket that only covers all the things you already know so well. Look there! Those are your favorite toys on the floor and the pillow you like to sit on when you watch TV," said the fairy. Jacob immediately saw that he was right. He grabbed his remote-controlled airplane from the floor and started playing with it, forgetting all his fears.

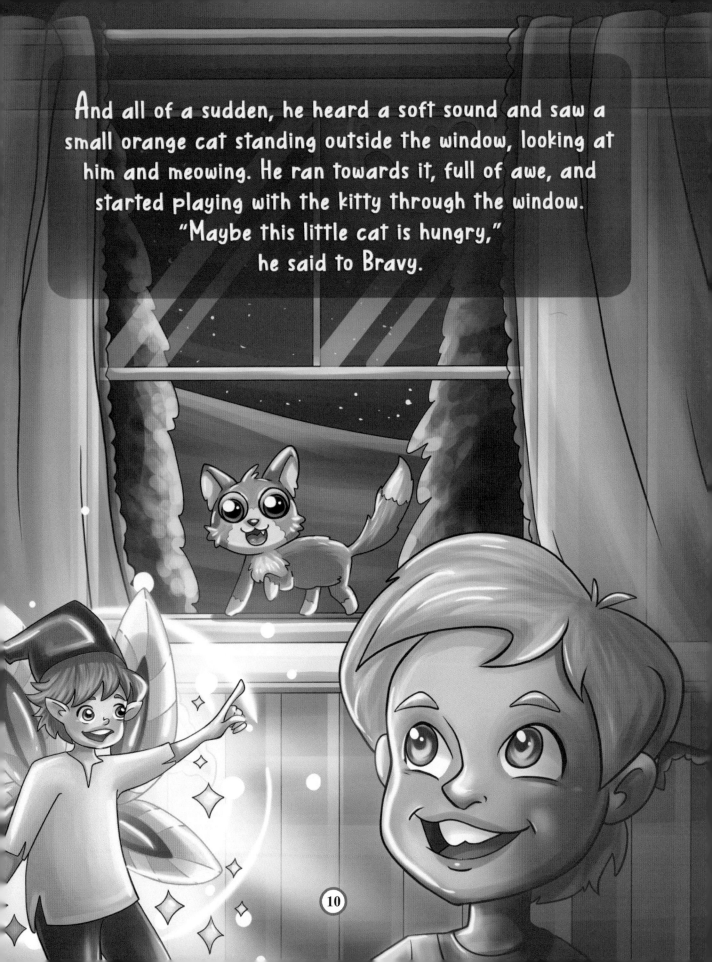

And all of a sudden, he heard a soft sound and saw a small orange cat standing outside the window, looking at him and meowing. He ran towards it, full of awe, and started playing with the kitty through the window. "Maybe this little cat is hungry," he said to Bravy.

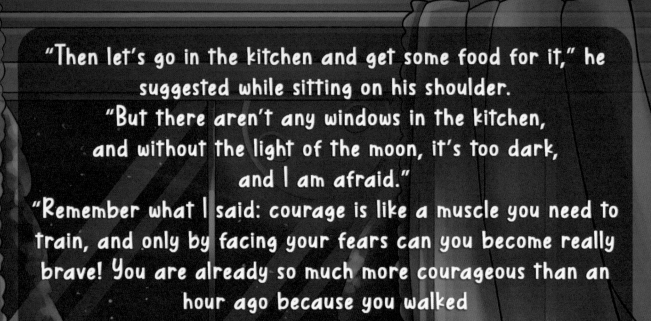

"Then let's go in the kitchen and get some food for it," he suggested while sitting on his shoulder.
"But there aren't any windows in the kitchen, and without the light of the moon, it's too dark, and I am afraid."
"Remember what I said: courage is like a muscle you need to train, and only by facing your fears can you become really brave! You are already so much more courageous than an hour ago because you walked with me all the way to the living room."

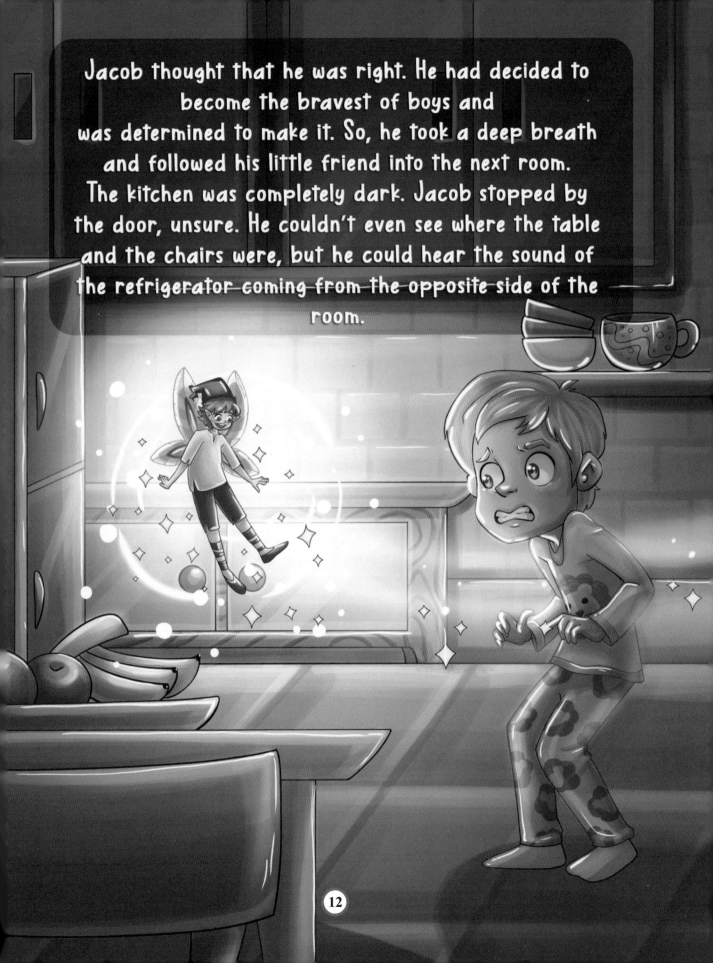

Jacob thought that he was right. He had decided to become the bravest of boys and was determined to make it. So, he took a deep breath and followed his little friend into the next room. The kitchen was completely dark. Jacob stopped by the door, unsure. He couldn't even see where the table and the chairs were, but he could hear the sound of the refrigerator coming from the opposite side of the room.

"Bravy," he said. "In the fridge, there is some milk I want to give to the kitty, but it is on the other side of the room, and I don't know how to get there."

" We will walk one step at a time, as we did before. And every step you will become," the fairy told him.

13

Jacob was still uncertain.
"Will you light the way for me again?"
"Of course! You don't have to face your fears all alone;
I am here to help you every time you need it." And
immediately, he flew in front of him, illuminating a clear
path to reach the fridge.
Jacob smiled, feeling more confident now, and ran to
the fridge to get the milk for the cat.

When he was nearly back to
the door, he remembered something.
"Oh! Wait here for me, Bravy. I will be right back!"
And without hesitation, he walked back into the dark room
towards the cupboard, where he remembered his
grandmother had stored some chocolate cookies. He
grabbed two, one for him and one for his new friend, and
found his way back to the living room.

"I am proud of you," the fairy told him while chewing on the giant biscuit nearly twice his size. "Just a few minutes ago, you were too scared to walk alone into the kitchen, and now you are not anymore. As I told you, if you believe in yourself and keep trying, nothing will stop you, and your fears will slowly disappear!"

"I know now that with a little help and by being strong, I can also become braver!"

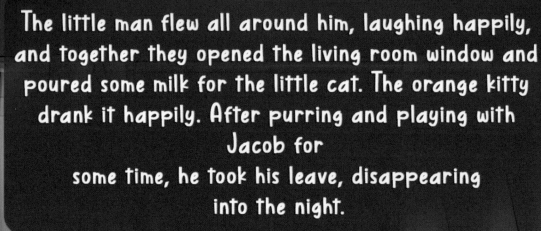

The little man flew all around him, laughing happily, and together they opened the living room window and poured some milk for the little cat. The orange kitty drank it happily. After purring and playing with Jacob for some time, he took his leave, disappearing into the night.

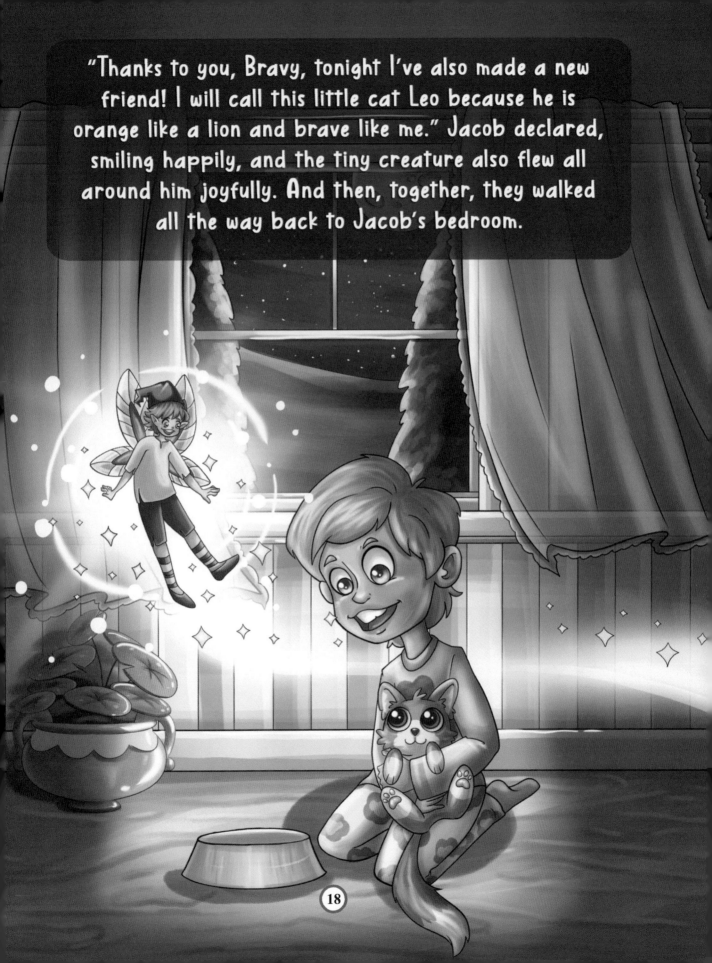

"Thanks to you, Bravy, tonight I've also made a new friend! I will call this little cat Leo because he is orange like a lion and brave like me." Jacob declared, smiling happily, and the tiny creature also flew all around him joyfully. And then, together, they walked all the way back to Jacob's bedroom.

Jacob wasn't scared anymore to walk in the darkness, and this time, he didn't even ask Bravy for help. Once he entered the bedroom, he ran to his bed and grabbed his teddy bear, hugging him hard and jumping around the room cheerfully. He then walked to his little desk, where paper and pencils were scattered around, and started drawing while sitting on the floor.

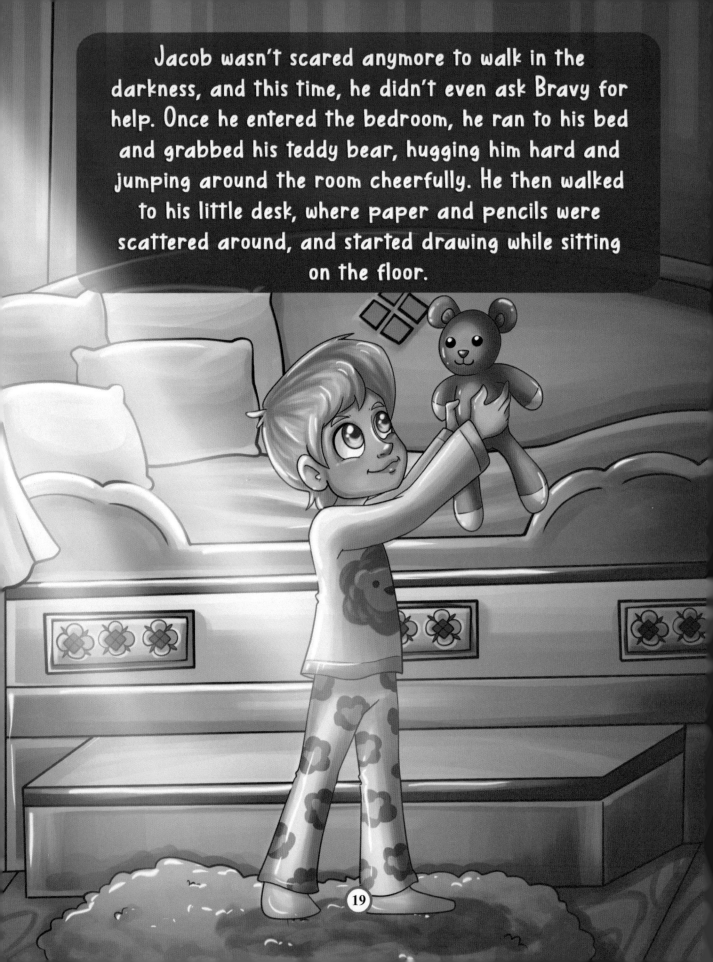

With yellow, green, and red pencils, he drew an image of his new little friend and himself and their amazing adventure together. He also sketched a drawing of Leo and the chocolate cookies they ate all together by the window. Once his artwork was finished, he called out for the fairy: "Bravy, Bravy! This is a gift for you to thank you for helping me become a brave boy!"

However, when he turned, the fairy was nowhere to be seen, and he realized he had been sitting in the darkness of the room for a long time. He called his name and looked in each corner of the bedroom for him, even inside the drawers and under the bed.
But there was no sign of the tiny creature. For a moment, he was sad that his friend was not with him anymore.

But then he realized that, after the incredible adventure they lived together and all the help he gave him to find courage, he would never forget about him, so, in a way, he would always be by his side. A big smile then came to his face, and he said out loud:

"Thank you, Bravy. Thank you for helping me find the courage to face my fears and become a brave kid. With your help, now, I am not afraid of the darkness anymore, and I can sleep alone at night peacefully. And if it wasn't for you, I wouldn't have met Leo and eaten those tasty chocolate cookies."

He then jumped into bed under the blankets and hugged his teddy bear. He was asleep nearly as soon as he closed his eyes and dreamed about the fantastic adventure he just lived and about his new curious and cheerful friend, who called himself the Guardian of Courage.

Summary of the Lessons
the Guardian Taught Jacob
About Bravery and Self-Empowerment

- Believe in yourself and your abilities; have faith that you can do whatever it takes to face any challenge.

- Take small steps towards conquering your fears; even if they seem overwhelming initially, breaking them down into smaller tasks will help make them more manageable.

- Don't be afraid to ask for help when needed; having a supportive team around you makes overcoming obstacles easier!

- Remember that courage is like a muscle—the more you use it, the stronger it gets!

- Have confidence in yourself and your own power to create change; you are the only one who can make a difference for yourself.

Questions for the Kids

1) What lessons did the Guardian teach Jacob about courage and self-empowerment?

Ans.

2) How can you use these lessons to help you face your fear of sleeping alone?

Ans.

3) Do any activities or rituals make you feel more comfortable in your bedroom before bed?

Ans.

4) What positive affirmations or mantras help empower you when feeling scared or anxious at bedtime?

Ans.

5) What are some ways to imagine yourself feeling safe and supported while sleeping alone?

Ans.

Examples of Answers:

1. Some of the lessons that the Guardian taught Jacob about courage and self-empowerment include believing in yourself, taking small steps towards conquering your fears, asking for help when needed, remembering that courage is like a muscle that gets stronger with use, and having confidence in your own power to create change.

2. To help face the fear of sleeping alone, you could take some slow deep breaths before going to bed to calm down any anxieties or worries; think about all the positive things that happened throughout the day as a reminder of how brave and capable you are; Make sure your bedroom is comfortable and inviting so it feels like a safe place; Talk out loud or write down any worries you have before falling asleep so they're not lingering on in your mind and keeping you awake; focus on calming activities such as reading or yoga poses beforehand – whatever helps relax your body!

3. Examples of activities or rituals that can make someone feel more comfortable in their bedroom before going to sleep include reading books, listening to calming music, writing down worries and thoughts on paper, snuggling up with a favorite stuffed animal or blanket, meditating on happy memories from earlier in the day.

4. Positive affirmations or mantras that can be used while feeling scared at bedtime include "I am safe," "I am strong," "I trust my intuition," "My fear does not define me," and "I am like a lion, and nothing can scare me!"

5. Some ways to imagine yourself feeling safe and supported when you're sleeping alone include imagining yourself surrounded by loved ones who care about you and support you no matter what—this could be family members/friends/pets; picturing yourself traveling through space with stars twinkling above—let these feelings wash over you until peacefulness takes over!

Tips for Parents to Help Their Kids Sleep

1. Establish a calming bedtime routine: create a series of simple steps to follow each night, such as taking a warm bath or shower, reading books, doing some light stretching or yoga poses, and brushing your teeth.

2. Put screens away at least an hour before bedtime; the blue light from phones and tablets can interfere with sleep cycles.

3. Make sure your child's bedroom is comfortable and relaxing; consider investing in blackout curtains to ensure total darkness during sleep time.

4. Keeping the room temperature cool—around 65–70 degrees Fahrenheit is ideal for sleeping comfortably through the night without waking up too hot or cold!

5. Give your child something comforting to hold onto while they drift off into dreamland; this could be anything from their favorite stuffed animal to a snuggly blanket.

Printed in Great Britain
by Amazon

42785124R00018